FABER has published children's books since 1929. T. S. Eliot's *Old Possum's Book of Practical Cats* and Ted Hughes' *The Iron Man* were amongst the first. Our catalogue at the time said that 'it is by reading such books that children learn the difference between the shoddy and the genuine'. We still believe in the power of reading to transform children's lives. All our books are chosen with the express intention of growing a love of reading, a thirst for knowledge and to cultivate empathy. We pride ourselves on responsible editing. Last but not least, we believe in kind and inclusive books in which all children feel represented and important.

About the Author

Francesca Simon is universally known for the staggeringly popular Horrid Henry series. She is also the author of Costa-shortlisted *The Monstrous Child*, which she turned into an opera with composer Gavin Higgins for the Royal Opera House, and two picture books: *Hack and Whack* and *The Goat Café*. She lives in North London with her family.

About the Illustrator

Steve May is an animation director and illustrator. Steve has illustrated books by Jeremy Strong, Philip Reeve, Harry Hill and Phil Earle, as well as the Dennis the Menace series. He lives in North London.

For Timothy Sheader and Paul Wills,
creators of stage magic.
F. S.

To Mum, Jackie and Andy – thanks for all
the absurdity!
S. M.

First published in 2021
by Faber & Faber Limited
Bloomsbury House,
74–77 Great Russell Street,
London WC1B 3DA
faberchildrens.co.uk
and
Profile Books
3 Holford Yard, Bevin Way,
London WC1X 9HD
www.profilebooks.com

This font has been specially chosen to support reading

Printed by CPI Group (UK) Ltd, Croydon CR0 4YY

All rights reserved

Text © Francesca Simon, 2021
Illustrations © Steve May, 2021

A CIP record for this book is available from the British Library

ISBN 978–0–571–34949–4

FSC
www.fsc.org
MIX
Paper from
responsible sources
FSC® C020471

2 4 6 8 10 9 7 5 3 1

FRANCESCA SIMON
Illustrated by Steve May

faber

PROFILE BOOKS

Characters

Hack

Whack

Bitey-Bitey

Twisty Pants

Dirty Ulf

Elsa Gold-Hair

Contents

ELSA GOLD-HAIR'S BIRTHDAY PARTY

'AAAARRRRRRGGGHHHH!'

'AAAARRRRRRGGGHHHH!'

'AAAARRRRRRGGGHHHH!'

Terrible screams came from the longhouse at the far end of the village.

Hack stopped swinging her sword.

Whack stopped swinging his axe.

Bitey-Bitey, their wolf cub, stopped chewing Dad's new leather boot.

ARRGGHH...

'That sounds like Dirty Ulf,' said Whack.

'AAAAARRRRRRRGGGHHH AARRRGHHH! HELP! HELP! Save me!'

'That **is** Dirty Ulf,' said Hack. She waved her sword. 'We have to rescue her.'

Whack waved his axe. 'It must be an ogre,' he yelled, running.

'Or a troll,' shouted Hack.

'We're Hack and Whack, on the attack!' they bellowed as

they raced across the turf towards the screams, leaping over chickens and crashing into goats. Bitey-Bitey ran after them, howling and yowling.

The blood-curdling shrieks seemed to be coming from a tub on the porch outside Dirty Ulf's longhouse. There was something gurgling and spluttering and squealing and splashing inside the black water.

Dirty Ulf's mother stood there,

clutching a bar of soap.

'Dirty Ulf is having a bath,' she said.

'I don't need a bath,' gasped Dirty Ulf, poking her head above the tub. 'I had one last year.'

Dirty Ulf's mum shoved her under the steaming water again.

'Why is she having a bath?' said Whack. Poor Dirty Ulf. No one hated water as much as she did.

'Because she is going to Elsa
Gold-Hair's birthday party,' said
her mum. 'And you know how
fussy those parents are.'

ARRRGGHH!

'Oh,' said Hack.

'Oh,' said Whack.

This was the first they had heard about a party.

'Now go away,' said Dirty Ulf's mother. 'Nothing to see here. Stop screaming, Dirty Ulf!' she screamed, attacking Ulf's ears with a spoon.

'NOOOOOOOOOOOOO,' howled Dirty Ulf.

Hack and Whack headed home.

'What's a birthday party?' said Hack.

'I don't know,' said Whack.

'Birth-day. Birth-day. The day you're born? Why would you have a party for that?'

Whack shrugged. 'Elsa is weird.'

Elsa liked sharing. Elsa liked playing quietly. Elsa liked telling everyone how naughty they were. Elsa thought she was a grown-up.

'Well, I don't want to go,' said Hack.

'Me neither,' said Whack. 'It would probably be really boring.'

'Really, really boring,' said Hack. 'Lucky we weren't invited.'

'Yeah,' said Whack. 'Lucky.'

Hack and Whack were just about to enter their longhouse when they heard loud voices coming from within.

Hack put a finger to her lips.

'Mum and Dad are talking about us,' she hissed.

Hack and Whack crept close to the wattled wall next to the woodpile and cupped their ears.

'Hack and Whack are the worst Vikings in the village,' said Mum.

'The very worst,' said Dad.

Hack and Whack beamed.

'But at least they're not like Elsa Gold-Hair.'

'Thank Thor,' said Dad. 'I

would die of shame to have such a goody-goody butter-face, hoity-toity salmon-flapper as **my** daughter.'

'Gods forbid,' said Mum.

'Did you hear, they caught her **sharing** last week?' said Dad.

'**Sharing?** No! Her poor parents.'

'Yes, sharing. Bragi Bread-Nose saw her. That girl will come to a bad end,' said Dad.

'Glad she's not our daughter,' said Mum. 'I blame the parents.'

'Not like us — firm but fair,' said Dad.

'Elsa's a terrible example. Thank Thor Hack and Whack weren't invited to her birthday party,' said Mum.

'I wouldn't let them go even if they **had** been invited. Elsa Gold-Hair might influence them, and the next thing we'd know, they'd stop fighting and quarrelling and playing with their swords.'

Hack and Whack had heard enough. Mum and Dad **didn't** want them to go?

'We want to go to Elsa's birthday party!' they yelled, bursting through the door.

'You can't. You weren't invited,'
said Dad.

'Why didn't she invite us?'

'Because you're the worst
Vikings in the village,' said Mum.
'Now go feed the chickens and
then help me churn the butter.'

Hack scowled.

'Mum, what happens at a birthday party?' said Whack.

Mum paused. 'I don't know,' she said. 'I think it's like some kind of feast.'

'Oooh,' said Hack.

'And I think the birthday child gets gifts . . .'

'. . . which we could steal,' whooped Whack.

'No stealing,' said Mum. 'You steal from the people on Bad Island, not from here. And we don't call it stealing. It's called raiding.'

Hack and Whack nodded. Raiding, not stealing.

Trudging their way to the

chicken coop they saw Black
Tooth, Spear Nose, Scar Leg,
Dirty Ulf, Little Sparrow, Twisty
Pants, Loud Mouth and Red
Cheek all heading towards
Elsa's home. Everyone carried
something in little pouches.

'We're going to Elsa's
party!' yelled Black
Tooth. 'C'mon.'

'We haven't
been invited,'
said Hack.

'So what?' said Twisty Pants.

'Come anyway,' said Dirty Ulf.

Hack and Whack looked at each other. Bitey-Bitey howled.

'Do you think we should go?' asked Whack.

'Yes,' said Hack. 'Who needs an invitation? It won't be a party without us.'

'We're coming!' yelled Hack and Whack.

The young Vikings banged on Elsa's door. She opened it,

wearing a new horse-shaped brooch attached to a bright blue cloak.

Elsa Gold-Hair was surprised to see Hack and Whack at her door.

Elsa Gold-Hair had definitely not invited them.

Elsa Gold-Hair was absolutely positive she hadn't invited them.

But Elsa Gold-Hair decided she was too grown up to make a fuss, so she welcomed everyone inside.

A warm fire burned low in the hearth. Loaves of bread were baking on the griddle set over the hot ashes. There were cushions and wall hangings and lots of carved stools. All the children except Hack and Whack brought

Elsa gifts of needles and fish hooks and arm-rings and flint and balls of wool and a Thor amulet. Dirty Ulf gave her the bone comb that belonged to her mother. 'No more hair combing without a comb,' she whispered to Hack and Whack.

Wow, what a hoard. Hack and Whack had never seen so many great gifts. They couldn't wait for Elsa to give them gifts in return.

They waited. And waited. And waited. But Elsa just kept admiring her treasure.

Hack and Whack couldn't believe their eyes. Why should one person get all the gifts? Was this any way to treat honoured guests?

No, it was not.

'Where are **our** gifts?' said Whack finally.

'Only the birthday girl gets presents,' said Elsa's mother,

Helga Gold-Hair.

'But **why** does Elsa get all the presents?' said Hack.

'Because it's **my** birthday,' said Elsa.

'But I'm a guest and I want a present,' said Whack.

'We want **all** the presents!' howled Hack and Whack.

'That's naughty,' said Elsa. 'You can't have them.'

'Don't you know that **I want doesn't get**?' said Elsa's mum.

'I want **always** gets,' said Whack.

'Not in this house,' said Elsa's dad. 'Here we take turns and share.'

Hack looked at Whack.

Whack looked at Hack.

Take turns? Share? Huh? What were they talking about?

'When do we sword fight?' asked Hack.

'That's naughty,' said Elsa. 'No sword fighting.'

'Where are the axes?' said Whack.

'No axes,' said Elsa. 'That's naughty.'

'When do we start throwing chicken bones at each other?' yelled Loud Mouth.

'No throwing food,' said Elsa. 'That's naughty.'

What kind of party was this?

'So what **ARE** we going to do?' shouted Hack and Whack. If only they could raid Elsa's presents . . . in fact it was their Viking **duty** to raid Elsa's presents. Hack inched closer to the glittering pile of gifts, twinkling on the wooden chest against the wall.

Elsa's father, Erik Gold-Hair,

climbed onto a bench right in front of the treasure. Hack froze.

'Listen, everyone. This is the first time we have ever had a birthday party in our village. And now we are going to play lots of fun games.'

'Sword fight!' shouted Whack.

'Food fight!' yelled Hack.

Helga Gold-Hair glared at them.

'First we're going to play pass the fish head,' said Helga.

'Everyone sit in a circle.'

Who'd want to pass around a fish head? Yuck.

'I wish I was at home washing clothes,' whispered Hack.

'Me too,' whispered Whack. 'Even digging for leeks would

be more fun than this.'

'Why are we passing round a fish head? It's bad enough gutting fish at home,' yelled Loud Mouth.

'Because the last one holding the fish head when the singing stops gets a prize,' said Erik Gold-Hair.

'Oooh,' said Twisty Pants and Loud Mouth.

'That's more like it,' said Spear Nose. She'd pass around

a hundred fish heads if it meant getting a prize.

The Vikings passed the fish head around the circle while Eric and Helga sang. It was a song they had made up themselves.

Oh, I'm a Viking, tra la la
Yo ho yo ho yo ho!
But that doesn't mean that
I can't share
So wipe away that frosty glare
Yo ho yo ho yo ho!
What's mine is yours,

what's yours is mine
Let's work together rain or
shine.
Yo ho yo—

Suddenly they stopped singing. Twisty Pants was holding the stinky fish head. Hack snatched it from him.

'Hey!' screeched Twisty Pants. 'Give that back.'

'No way,' said Hack, dancing off.

'Give it back,' said Erik Gold-Hair.

'You said whoever was **holding** the fish head got the prize,' said Hack. 'And I'm holding it.'

Twisty Pants snatched the head back.

'Mine!' he screamed.

'Mine!' screamed Hack,

snatching it back as it slid from her hands, bounced across the room and flew SMACK into Elsa Gold-Hair's face.

'Aaaarrrggghhhh!' squealed Elsa.

'No prize,' said Erik Gold-Hair.

'I want the prize!' screamed Hack and Twisty Pants.

'I want doesn't get,' said Erik Gold-Hair. 'Let's try something else. Let's play pin the tail on the ogre, and—'

'Where's the ogre?' shouted Whack. Wow, a real ogre. He wondered where they were hiding it.

'Won't we get eaten?' said Spear Nose.

'It's not a real ogre,' said Erik. 'I drew one on this piece of linen.'

Oh.

Elsa sighed.

'Boring,' yelled Hack.

Erik ignored her.

Helga tied a piece of cloth around their eyes in turn, and the Vikings tried to pin the tail on the ogre. Except for Hack and Whack who pinned the tail on Elsa accidentally on purpose.

Scar Leg came closest. His prize was a ball of wool.

Hack and Whack yawned. They thought they would die of boredom.

'I wish I was at home gutting fish,' muttered Hack.

'I wish I was at home untangling wool,' muttered Whack.

'I wish — oh, I **am** at home,' said Elsa.

'Come on, Elsa, let's play . . .

frozen troll!' said Erik.

Frozen troll? Hack and Whack perked up. **Finally**, a fun game.

'Are we going to trap a troll?' said Hack. Wow, Elsa's birthday party was suddenly turning out to be much better than she thought.

'No,' said Elsa. 'That's naughty. Frozen troll is a game. Everyone dances until Mum yells "frozen troll" and then you have to stand still. The first person who moves loses, and then we do it again till there is only one little troll standing.'

'Oh,' said Hack.

'Oh,' said Whack.

Helga took out her recorder and began to play.

'Dance, everyone,' said Erik.

Hack started to dance. Whack danced next to her. They moved closer and closer and closer to the chest where Elsa's presents were heaped.

Then . . . SNATCH! Elsa's fish hooks and amulet vanished inside Hack's pouch.

Whack danced wildly next to the chest. He reached behind and . . . SNATCH! Elsa's flint and

needles and arm-rings vanished inside **his** pouch.

'Let's play . . . raiding,' shouted Hack.

'Yeah,' said Whack.

'Yeah,' yelled Twisty Pants, Loud Mouth and Dirty Ulf, pulling out their wooden swords and axes, and hacking and whacking.

They jumped on to the table, knocking over the drinking horns and knives.

'We're Hack and Whack, on

the attack!'

'If you can't play nicely, get out!' screeched Helga.

Hack and Whack didn't wait to be asked twice and ran outside. Bitey-Bitey whined when he saw them. He was jumping up and trying to catch a fish drying on a rack in the yard. He jumped and jumped but the fish were hanging too high above his head.

'Bitey-Bitey's hungry,' said Whack. 'He hasn't eaten since

breakfast and it's almost lunch.'

'Poor Bitey-Bitey,' said Hack.

'Poor Bitey-Bitey,' said Whack.

Hack reached up, snatched a fish from the hook and threw it to Bitey-Bitey. Bitey-Bitey wolfed it down.

'He's still hungry,' said Whack.

Hack unhooked another fish. Then another. And another.

Gulp. Chomp.

Gulp. Chomp.

Gulp. Chomp.

Until all the fish were gone.

Helga Gold-Hair appeared at the door. 'Now, Hack and Whack, if you promise to behave, you can come back inside and play— My fish! My lovely fish!' shrieked Helga. 'You wicked wolf! That's it. Go home, Hack.

Go home, Whack. Just wait till I tell your parents about your behaviour.'

Uh-oh. Uh-oh. Their parents had forbidden them to go to Elsa's party.

'We're going to be punished,' howled Hack.

'Oh no,' wailed Whack.

'They'll shut us in the chicken coop for a week.'

'They'll make us sleep with the pigs.'

'They'll send us to the forest forever!'

'We'll be eating whale blubber for a year!'

'We're doomed!' shrieked Hack and Whack.

Shivering and quivering, shaking and quaking, Hack and Whack crept home.

'Where have you been?' shouted their mother. 'Have you fed the chickens?'

'No,' said Hack.

'Have you churned the butter?'

'No,' said Whack.

'So what have you been doing?'

'Ummm,' said Hack.

'You see . . .' said Whack.

Hack reached into her pouch and took out the fish hooks and the amulet.

Whack reached into his pouch and took out the flint and needles and arm-rings.

'What's all this?' said Dad.

'We raided Elsa Gold-Hair's presents,' said Hack.

'You **raided** Elsa's presents? After I told you that you can only raid Bad Island?' shouted Mum.

Hack hung her head.

Whack hung his head.

They were dead meat.

'You're the worst Vikings in the village,' said Mum.

'Yes, you are,' said Dad. 'The very worst.'

'Which makes us the **best** Viking parents in the village!' said Mum. 'I think we should have a feast to celebrate!'

TWO TERRIBLE
VIKINGS TRACK
A TROLL

Thwack! A snowball smacked
Olga Fish-Belly in the face.

'Aaaaarrrggghhh!' shrieked
Olga Fish-Belly. 'Who did that?'

Thwack! A snowball smacked

Hildi Horn-Head in the back.

'Aaaaaaarrrggghh!' shrieked Hildi Horn-Head. 'Who did that?'

Thwack! Thwack! Two snowballs smacked Bragi Bread-Nose on the bottom.

'Owwwwwww!' yowled Bragi Bread-Nose. 'Owwwwww!'

'Gotcha! Gotcha! Gotcha!' shrieked Hack and Whack.

'OWWWWWWWWWW!' yelled Bragi Bread-Nose, grabbing his bum. 'Just wait till I get my hands on you, you herring-breath hooligans. I'll throw you in a ghost-pit. And your wolf-pup too.'

'Gotcha! Gotcha! Gotcha!' shrieked Hack and Whack.

They ran off, laughing and cheering. 'We're Hack and Whack, on the attack!'

'You're the worst Vikings in the village,' shouted Hildi Horn-Head.

'The very, very worst,' shouted Bragi Bread-Nose.

'Yay,' cheered Hack and Whack. They liked being the best at something. Especially if it was being the best at being the worst.

'I hope the trolls take you,' shouted Olga Fish-Belly.

'We're too tough for trolls,' said Hack, sticking out her tongue.

'We're too fast for trolls,' said Whack, blowing a raspberry.

'We're too clever for trolls,' yelled Hack and Whack.

Hack chased Whack round the yard and crashed into the rainwater barrels. The chickens scattered, squawking. Bitey-

Bitey ran after them, howling.

The goat on the grass roof
stopped nibbling and stared.

Then Hack pinched Whack.

Whack pulled Hack's plaits.

Hack knocked Whack's helmet off his head. And kicked him.

Whack ran.

'Gotcha!' shrieked Hack.

'No! I got you!' shrieked Whack.

'Didn't!'

'Did!'

Whack sniffed.

'Do you smell burning?' he said.

Hack sniffed.

'I do,' she said.

'What could it be?' said Whack. 'It's not coming from our house, is it?'

Hack looked at Whack.

Whack looked at Hack.

Uh-oh.

Uh-oh. Uh-oh. Uh-oh.

Hack and Whack ran inside their longhouse. Smoke was pouring from the iron cauldron suspended over the fire in the middle of the room.

Mum came running in. She

grabbed a bucket of water and poured it into the cauldron, which hissed and steamed, belching black smoke. 'Who let the porridge burn? I put you two in charge of stirring it.'

Whack pointed at Hack. 'She did,' said Whack, coughing.

Hack pointed at Whack. 'He did,' said Hack, coughing.

Mum stomped towards them. Her hands were covered in raw dough.

'Hack! Whack!' screamed Mum. 'Go to Trollwood and fetch some firewood NOW. And dig up some leeks while you're at it. We're running low. And watch out for bears. They're mean and hungry this time of year.'

'But,' said Hack.

'But . . .' said Whack.

'No ifs, no buts,' said Mum. 'I've had just about enough of you two today. Now get a move on. And don't you dare lose your mittens again. You know how long it took me to make them.'

Hack opened her mouth to shout back, then she saw Olga Fish-Belly, Hildi Horn-Head, and

Bragi Bread-Nose stomping towards the house. She grabbed Whack's tunic.

'Okay, Mum,' she said, dragging her brother out the door and scampering through the cowshed.

'Hurry up,' said Mum, calling after them. 'We need to start smoking the fish today. And the wool is in a terrible tangle. Hello, Bread-Nose, hello, Fish-Belly, Hello, Horn-Head, what brings you all the way here—'

Hack and Whack ran through the village, dodging chickens and goats. Then they entered the dark and gloomy forest of Trollwood. The light sprinkling of snow crunched under their boots. Bitey-Bitey ran ahead, chasing foxes.

'Leeks,' muttered Hack. 'I hate leeks.'

'Leeks taste like mud,' said Whack.

'Leeks taste even worse than whale blubber,' said Hack.

'Nothing tastes worse than whale blubber,' said Whack.

'Maybe we can find some strawberries instead,' said Hack.

'It's too cold for strawberries,' said Whack.

Hack sighed.

They continued walking through the forest, trudging along the stony path that wove through the snow-covered birch trees and slippery moss. They breathed in the earthy smell of wet bracken.

'I'm not seeing any firewood,' said Hack, kicking away a bramble. Far off in the distance, a raven cawed.

'We'll have to go further in,' said Whack, skipping over a bubbly, flint-grey stream fed by a thundering waterfall.

'Mum and Dad should be collecting firewood, not us,' said

Hack. She thought for a moment about the warm fire in their longhouse. 'Why do we have to do so many chores? It's not fair.'

'Just wait, the moment we get back she'll have us darning socks and gutting fish,' said Whack.

'ICK!'

'YUCK!'

'GROSS!'

Hack and Whack ploughed deeper into the dark, damp woods. Ravens shrieked and circled above their heads. The freezing mist made them shiver inside their furs. All around them birch branches bent low, weighed down with snow.

'Why is this forest called Trollwood?' said Whack.

'Duh. Because trolls live here.'

'I'm not scared of trolls. Trolls are stupid,' said Whack.

'Yeah,' said Hack. 'We're much smarter than a troll. At least I am. I don't know about you.' She pushed him. Whack pushed her back.

'Stop,' said Hack. She pointed at the snowy path. 'Look.'

'Oh wow,' said Whack. 'Those are . . . those are . . .'

'Troll tracks! What else could they be?'

'Look how big they are,' said Whack, fitting his boot inside one of the enormous footprints.

'Let's follow them,' said Hack. 'I bet they'll lead us to their treasure hoard.'

'Oh yes,' said Whack. 'A troll

treasure hoard. Wouldn't it be great to find it?'

'We'd be the richest Vikings in the village,' said Hack. 'Let's go.'

Hack and Whack tracked the troll deeper and deeper into Trollwood. The icy air smelled clean and crisp and wet.

'Did you know the forest trolls have heads as high as trees?' said Hack, pushing her way through the ferns.

'Wrong. Heads as high as

mountains,' said Whack.

'Their shoulders are wider than valleys.'

'And the three-headed ones share an eye between them,' said Whack.

'There's a troll hag who carries her heads under her arms . . .'

'Which one do you think we're tracking?' asked Whack.

'Why?' said Hack. 'Are you scared?'

'Nah. You?'

'Nah. Bitey-Bitey? Are you scared?'

Bitey-Bitey growled.

'He's not scared either,' said Whack.

Bitey-Bitey began to howl, then ran off into the dense trees.

Just ahead came the sound of breaking branches.

Hack clutched Whack.

Whack clutched Hack.

'There's something in there,' whispered Hack.

'It's tearing up the forest,' whispered Whack.

'AWHOOOOOOOOOOO!' howled Bitey-Bitey.

'He's found something,' hissed Hack. She squared her shoulders. 'I'm going in after him.'

She marched off towards the birch trees.

'Don't leave me,' wailed Whack, running after her.

They stopped behind some bushes and peeked around the

side. In the clearing was a small figure yanking thin branches off a mossy, fallen tree.

'Oi, Twisty Pants,' yelled Hack.

'What are you doing, Twisty Pants?' yelled Whack.

The small figure straightened and tugged up his trousers.

'I'm fishing,' said Twisty Pants. 'What does it look like I'm doing? I'm collecting firewood.'

'Your parents should be doing that,' said Whack.

'What are you, a slave?' said Hack. 'Come with us, we're tracking trolls.'

Twisty Pants dropped the firewood. 'I'll come,' he said. 'Lucky you found me because

I've fought a troll before.'

'So have I,' said Hack. 'I charged at him with my sword . . .'

'. . . then he ran off into the forest,' said Whack.

'That's nothing,' bragged Twisty Pants. 'Once I sneaked up on a troll while he was snoring like all the waves in the world roaring together. Then I chopped off his head.'

'How big was it?' asked Hack.

'Big as a volcano,' said Twisty Pants.

'I think this one is bigger,' said Hack.

'Definitely,' said Whack.

Hack and Whack and Twisty Pants tracked the troll further into the woods. Its massive footprints were everywhere, stomping and trampling.

'There's definitely more than one, said Whack. 'Just look at all the other footprints.'

'Good thing I'm here to save the day,' said Twisty Pants.

'How many trolls do you think there are?' said Hack.

'Loads,' said Whack. 'And ogres too.'

'We can handle them,' said Hack. 'Ogres and trolls are stupid.'

A branch cracked.

The terrible Vikings froze.

'What's that noise?' whispered Whack, peering through the grey mist.

Hack listened. It sounded like something panting. Something gasping. Bitey-Bitey growled.

'It's the troll,' whispered Hack.

'It's lots of trolls,' whispered Whack.

Hack drew her sword.

Whack drew his axe.

Twisty Pants hid behind them.

Suddenly a snow-covered blob burst out from behind a tree.

Hack screamed.

Whack screamed.

'Hi,' said the blob, shaking itself.

'Dirty Ulf! What are you doing here?' gasped Hack.

'I've run away,' said Dirty Ulf.

'Why?'

'Mum wanted to comb my hair.'

'Oh,' said Hack.

'Ah,' said Whack.

Dirty Ulf hated having her hair combed almost as much as she hated baths.

'Why?'

'She wanted me to play at Elsa's house while she took some pigs to market,' said Dirty Ulf.

A comb **AND** stuck with boring goody-goody Elsa Gold-

Hair on the same day. That was a fate worse than death. A fate worse than falling into a volcano. A fate worse than being swallowed by a whale.

'You'd better come with us,' said Twisty Pants. 'We're tracking trolls.'

'Great,' said Dirty Ulf.

Snow began to fall harder as day sank into dusk. The forest turned into a glistening white world of shadow and rock. The giant footprints gleamed on the frosty path.

'See these footprints?' said Whack, pointing to the snowy path weaving between the trees.

'Trolls,' said Dirty Ulf. 'Definitely trolls. I'd recognise their prints anywhere. Once I saw a troll eating, and it had a spoon as big as a shovel.'

'That's nothing,' said Twisty Pants. 'When I saw a troll

eating, it had a fork bigger than a pitchfork.'

'When we saw two trolls eating they were making so

much noise it sounded like all the pigs in the world grunting and squealing,' said Hack.

'Yeah,' said Whack. 'You wouldn't believe the noise they made. Their drool was like a waterfall.'

The little Viking band paused beneath a massive stone

soaring out of a cliff.

'There's runes written on it,' said Hack. 'What does it say?'

'I can read,' said Dirty Ulf, pushing him aside. She squinted at the rune stone.

'It says, **BEWARE! Trolls**.'

Hack and Whack looked up at the stone. The big, huge,

enormous stone with the jagged tombstone teeth and the enormous troll belly. A troll

belly probably filled with little Vikings who went wandering in the woods and never came back.

Bitey-Bitey growled and howled.

'Pooh!' said Hack.

'Phooey!' said Whack.

'Gulp,' said Twisty Pants.

Twisty Pants began to wonder whether he'd be back in time for supper — for a roast lamb supper with mushrooms and nuts and barley bread and mead.

Dirty Ulf began to wonder if having her hair combed was really so bad.

'Trolls are dumb,' said Hack.

'If they were smart they wouldn't get turned to stone,' said Whack.

'We're much smarter than any troll,' said Hack.

'Yeah,' said Whack.

'Do you remember the story Fish-Belly told about the troll

who banged people flat and turned them into pancakes that he cooked for dinner?' whispered Dirty Ulf.

'What do you expect?' said Hack. 'Trolls are always hungry.'

'Was that the two-headed troll?' said Twisty Pants.

'Three-headed,' said Dirty Ulf.

'Are you scared, Twisty Pants?' said Hack. 'Because if you are you can go back to the village right now. Troll-tracking isn't for scaredy-cats.'

'Shut up,' hissed Whack. 'Look.'

Everyone gathered round and stared at the footprints. Now there were small ones mixed up with the giant ones.

'They've changed direction . . . We're not following them — the trolls are following us!' gasped Hack.

Suddenly there was the sound of heavy breathing coming from the dark trees behind them.

'Did you hear that?' said Dirty Ulf. 'That . . . that . . . snuffling noise . . .'

'You mean . . . that grunting and groaning noise?' said Hack.

'You mean . . . that snorting

and stomping?' said Whack.

'RUN!' shrieked Hack and Whack.

'Run for your life!' screamed Twisty Pants.

'It's trolls!' screamed Dirty Ulf.

'Awhoooooooooooooo,'
howled Bitey-Bitey.

The Vikings ran through the
forest. They did not stop until

they reached the edge of their village.

'Thor! That was close,' gasped Twisty Pants.

And then they heard the troll again . . .

'Help!' screamed Hack.

'Help!' screamed Whack.

'Help!' screamed Twisty Pants.

Something burst out of the darkness.

'Help! Help!' screamed Dirty Ulf.

The Viking band ran off screaming towards their homes, shrieking and wailing.

A snow-covered figure stumbled out from the trees.

It shook itself and icy flakes tumbled from its body.

Then it lifted one gigantic foot. And then the other.

'Hey, stop! That's naughty!' the voice bellowed. 'I only wanted to play,' shouted Elsa Gold-Hair. She shook the snow off her

enormous snow skis. 'Why did
you all run away?'

HACK AND WHACK
RAID BAD ISLAND

Hack and Whack sat on top of the woodpile next to their longhouse.

They watched their wolf cub Bitey-Bitey chase the pigs.

They watched the pigs chase Bitey-Bitey.

They watched Bitey-Bitey
chase the chickens.

They watched the chickens
chase Bitey-Bitey.

Hack yawned.

Whack yawned.

Bitey-Bitey sighed, scratched his grey head, curled up on Whack's feet and fell asleep. The young wolf smelled of firewood and something horrible he'd rolled in.

'I'm bored,' said Hack.

'I'm bored,' said Whack.

'We could pick berries,' said Hack.

'Nah,' said Whack. 'Too much

work.'

'We could scare the goats,' said Hack.

'Nah,' said Whack. 'We did that yesterday.'

'Hack! Whack!' shouted Mum. 'Where are you? You need to do your chores. Now.'

'Chores?' said Hack.

'Chores?' said Whack.

'Nooooooooooo!' said Hack and Whack.

Mum came round the side of

the longhouse.

'Get down from there, you lazy lumps,' said Mum. 'You need to:

fetch water,

feed the chickens,

find the eggs,

churn the butter,

grind the wheat,

knead the bread,

gather mushrooms,

and make it snappy, Hack and Whack! Then you need to unknot all the wool you tangled, clean

the stable and—'

Hack looked at Whack.

Whack looked at Hack.

What was this, cruelty to children? Why was their mother so lazy?

'Run!' shouted Hack and Whack. They jumped off the woodpile and raced down the hill towards the shore. Bitey-Bitey followed them, howling joyfully.

'Hack and Whack! Come back. You have to do your chores!' screamed Mum.

'We're free!' shouted Hack.

'We're Hack and Whack, on the attack!' shouted Whack.

'Let's have an adventure,' said Hack.

'Yeah! Let's do something brave and daring,' said Whack.

'Let's do something we've been told to never, ever do,' said Hack.

'Yeah,' said Whack.

They thought.

And then Hack had the most wonderful, thrilling and terrifying idea.

'Let's raid Bad Island,' said Hack.

Whack stared at his twin.

Why hadn't **he** thought of that?

'Oh yes,' said Whack. 'We can steal swords.'

'And axes.'

'And shields.'

'And gold.'

'Lots and lots and lots of gold.'

'What are we waiting for? Let's go!'

Hack and Whack ran to the water's edge where big boats and small boats had been pulled onto the beach.

Twisty Pants and Dirty Ulf were standing barefoot on the wet black sand, skimming stones into the waves. Elsa Gold-Hair stood a little way off, watching them. She was clutching a big basket of mushrooms. Far off on the horizon, immense blue-grey glaciers glistened.

'We're going raiding,' yelled Hack.

Twisty Pants dropped his

stones and straightened his woollen jerkin.

'Lucky you found me,' he said. 'I've been raiding loads of times.'

Dirty Ulf pulled on her fur-lined boots.

'You'll need me too,' said Dirty Ulf. 'I always find the best treasure.'

'Join us,' said Whack. 'You can help carry all the loot we're going to steal from Bad Island.'

'Hey!' said Elsa Gold-Hair. 'That's naughty! We're too young to go raiding. Even King Olaf was twelve when he first went.'

'What a slow-boat,' said Hack.

'I'm in,' said Dirty Ulf. 'Just so long as I don't have to have a bath.'

'Raiders don't need baths,' said Whack.

'Phew,' said Dirty Ulf.

'I'm not going raiding,' said Elsa. 'I still have chores to do.'

'You'll miss all the fun,' said Twisty Pants.

'I don't want to get in trouble,' said Elsa.

Hack stopped in front of a small sailboat. It had two wide seats and two oars.

'Nice boat,' said Hack.

'VERY nice boat,' said Whack.

'Perfect for raiding,' said Dirty Ulf.

'It's smaller than **my** raiding boat,' said Twisty Pants. 'But it will do.'

Hack, Whack, Dirty Ulf and Twisty Pants grabbed the rowboat and pushed it into the choppy water.

'Last chance, Elsa,' said Whack.

Bitey-Bitey jumped into the boat, howling.

'Hack, Whack, leave my boat alone,' shouted Sven Fork-Beard, running down the beach towards them.

'Uh-oh,' said Dirty Ulf.

Elsa froze. She looked at Sven. Then she looked at the raiders scrambling into the boat.

'I'll tear you all limb from limb!' screamed Sven, charging.

Elsa shrieked, dropped her

basket and ran to the boat. Dirty
Ulf and Twisty Pants pulled her
in as Sven splashed into the icy
water after them.

'Get back here!'

'Row for your life!' shouted

Twisty Pants.

Hack and Whack grabbed one oar and Dirty Ulf and Twisty Pants the other.

'Row!' squealed Whack.

'Put up the sail!' squealed Hack.

Hack grabbed the oar from Whack. 'I can steer. You put up the sail.'

'No, I'll steer,' said Whack. 'You put up the sail.'

'You're doing it wrong,' said Hack.

'**You're** doing it wrong,' said Whack.

The little boat spun round and round and round.

'Wheeeee!' said Hack and Whack.

'Wheeeee!' said Twisty Pants and Dirty Ulf.

'Help!' squealed Elsa Gold-Hair.

The boat whacked Sven and he toppled into the grey water.

Splash!

'Just wait till I tell your parents,' shrieked Sven, shaking his fist at them.

'Row! Row! As fast as you can. We're going raiding!' screamed Hack.

The oars slapped into the choppy sea.

Hack and Whack and Dirty Ulf and Twisty Pants rowed and rowed and rowed.

'We're going raiding,' sang Hack and Whack.

'A pirate's life for me,' sang Twisty Pants and Dirty Ulf.

The wind filled their sail, speeding them along.

'I'm going to be in so much trouble,' said Elsa.

'Which way to Bad Island?' said Hack.

'That way!' shouted Twisty Pants. He pointed left.

'Sure?' said Hack.

'Of course I'm sure,' said Twisty Pants. 'I've been raiding

loads of times and we always head that-a-way.'

'Watch out, Bad Island, here come Hack and Whack, on the attack!'

'You won't stand a chance against Twisty Pants,' shouted Twisty Pants.

'That doesn't rhyme,' said Elsa.

'Who cares?' said Twisty Pants.

'Hack and Whack rule the waves,' shouted Hack.

'Whack and Hack are on the attack!' shouted Whack.

The terrible Viking twins smiled at each other.

'Beware, it's Elsa Gold-Hair,' whispered Elsa.

'Beware, it's Elsa Gold-Hair,' said Elsa.

'BEWARE, IT'S ELSA GOLD-HAIR!' shrieked Elsa.

'BEWARE, IT'S ELSA GOLD-HAIR!' shrieked Hack, Whack, Twisty Pants and Dirty

Ulf.

'Did I ever tell you about the time I fought a sea monster?' said Twisty Pants.

'A million times,' said Dirty Ulf.

Twisty Pants frowned.

'At least I've seen one, which is more than **you** have,' said Twisty Pants. 'And I whacked it on its heads with my oar. Lucky I was there to save the day.'

They rowed. And they rowed. And they rowed and they rowed and they rowed and rowed and rowed until their hands ached and their backs ached and their heads ached. Even the sight of a pod of whales leaping out of the sea and crashing down with huge splashes didn't lift their spirits.

'Which way now?' said Hack. She hadn't realised raiding would be such hard, heavy work.

'That way,' said Twisty Pants. He pointed right. 'Lucky I'm here to save the day.'

They rowed. And they rowed. And they rowed and they rowed and they rowed and rowed and rowed.

'Phew,' said Dirty Ulf.

'It's a long way to Bad Island,' said Hack.

'I didn't know it was so far away,' said Whack.

'I could have told you **that**,' said Twisty Pants.

'You know that Bad Island has ogres and giants and trolls,' said Elsa.

'So what?' said Whack.

'I've fought trolls and tricked giants loads of times,' said

Twisty Pants.

'And the Bad Island Vikings are the fiercest warriors in the world.'

'I'm not scared,' said Whack. 'I'm never scared. Are **you** scared?'

'No way,' said Hack.

'No way,' said Twisty Pants.

'No way,' said Dirty Ulf. 'As long as they don't attack me with a comb.'

'Look, up ahead,' said Whack.

'Do you see what I see?'

'Bad Island!' said Hack. 'We're here.'

'Land ahoy!' said Dirty Ulf.

'Told you,' said Twisty Pants.

'At last,' said Hack. 'My arms hurt.'

'My legs hurt,' said Whack.

'My hands hurt,' said Dirty Ulf.

'My arms **and** legs **and** hands

hurt,' said Twisty Pants.

Elsa opened her mouth to say that she was cold and wet but as she hadn't done any rowing, she decided to keep quiet.

'But just think of all the treasure we'll be raiding,' said Whack.

'Yeah,' said Hack. 'Bad Island is stuffed with gold. They eat off gold plates.'

'They drink from silver cups,' said Twisty Pants. 'I know

'cause I found some on my **last** raid there.'

'I've heard even their buckets and barrels are made of gold,' said Dirty Ulf.

'I don't want a gold bucket,' said Whack. 'I'm grabbing as many axes as I can carry.'

'I'm grabbing as many helmets as I can carry,' said Hack.

'And silver swords,' said Twisty Pants.

'I can't wait to snatch all that

treasure,' said Dirty Ulf.

'We'll be the richest Vikings in the world,' said Whack.

'Mum and Dad will be so proud,' said Hack.

'And Loud Mouth and Spear Nose will be spitting with envy when we stroll around wearing our gold arm-rings and waving our silver swords,' said Dirty Ulf.

'And gold brooches and drinking horns. Don't forget them,' said Twisty Pants.

'What should we buy with all our loot?' said Whack.

Hack thought. 'I think . . . I think we should buy . . . a whale.'

'We can't keep a whale,' said Whack.

'Okay, then snow skis like Elsa's.'

'Yeah,' said Whack. 'Snow skis.' Elsa Gold-Hair had the biggest and best snow skis in the village.

'You can borrow my skis,' said Elsa.

'Oh wow,' said Hack. 'Really?'

'Really,' said Elsa.

'I still want my own,' said

Whack.

'Obviously,' said Hack. 'But thank you, Elsa.'

The Viking band rowed closer and closer to the shore. The waves pushed them into the sheltered harbour. They jumped out of the boat and crept up the beach. Bitey-Bitey followed, sniffing and bouncing on the black sand.

'Bad Island looks huge,' whispered Dirty Ulf.

'It **is** huge,' said Hack.

'Do you see any giants?' said Whack.

'Not yet,' said Hack.

'Do you see any trolls?' said Twisty Pants.

'Not yet,' said Hack.

'How about ogres?' said Elsa Gold-Hair.

'Not yet,' said Hack.

'I see a village,' whispered Whack. 'Up on the hill.'

'Let's sneak up on it,' said

Hack.

Hack and Whack and Twisty Pants and Dirty Ulf and Elsa Gold-Hair tugged their sailboat onto the shore.

'Look out for giants,' said Hack.

'And ogres,' said Elsa.

'And trolls,' said Twisty Pants.

Elsa stood still. She was scared to stay and scared to move.

'I don't want to go raiding,'

she said, even though she would have quite liked a bracelet. Or even a shield.

'Then stay and guard the boat,' said Hack, waving her sword.

Whack pulled out his axe.

Dirty Ulf drew her sword.

Twisty Pants grabbed his axe.

Bitey-Bitey growled low in his throat.

'Shh,' said Whack. 'Good wolf. I'll tell you when to attack, Bitey-Bitey.'

Bitey-Bitey licked his face.

'Ready?' said Hack.

'Ready!'

'Ready!'

'Ready!'

'Then let's raid!' said Hack.

Sneak.

Sneak.

Sneak.

The fearless band of Viking raiders crept up the beach towards the village. Smoke drifted from the smoke holes in the centre of every thatched roof. Goats wandered between the longhouses. Fish dried on hooks. Bread cooked on fires. Chickens ran around squawking. The sound of a blacksmith hammering drifted down.

'Isn't it strange?' said Hack. 'I thought there would be glaciers and mountains and volcanoes on Bad Island.'

'It's just hills and trees,' said Dirty Ulf.

'And there's a stream just like the one near us,' said Whack.

The Vikings, followed by Bitey-Bitey, splashed through

the stream.

'Shh,' said Hack.

'Shh,' said Whack.

'Awhoooooooooo!' howled Bitey-Bitey.

'Let's go to the biggest longhouse,' said Whack. 'They'll have the most gold.'

'I love gold,' said Hack.

'Me too,' said Whack.

'Me too,' said Dirty Ulf.

'Me too,' said Twisty Pants.

Tiptoe.

Tiptoe.

Tiptoe.

Bitey-Bitey growled a warning.

'Shhh, Bitey-Bitey,' hissed Hack.

Then they heard footsteps. Someone was coming.

'Hide,' squeaked Whack. They all hid behind some rain barrels.

The footsteps walked past them.

'Phew,' said Whack.

'Close call,' said Hack.

'What about that longhouse?' whispered Whack. He pointed to one that stood a little apart from the others. 'Bet they've got loads of treasure.'

'What if someone is in there?' said Twisty Pants. He looked pale.

'Bah,' said Whack. 'We'll scare them off.'

The Vikings peeked round the door. The longhouse was empty.

'Hurrah!'

Hack and Whack ran to the chest in the corner. They flung open the lid. It was filled with furs and brooches and buckles and neck-rings.

'Wow,' said Hack.

'Wow,' said Whack.

They scooped up as much jewellery as they could carry, then piled it on the wooden table.

'We're raiders,' said Hack.

'We're real raiders,' said Whack.

'People will tell sagas and write songs about me,' said Twisty Pants, nabbing spears.

'About **us**,' said Dirty Ulf, snatching swords off the walls.

'I can't reach that shield,' said

Hack. 'It's too high.'

Hack and Whack grabbed a stool.

Hack stood on tiptoe.

'Almost . . . almost . . . got it,' she said, as her fingers brushed the huge shield.

CLANG!

BASH!

CRASH!

The stool tipped over. Hack and Whack clattered to the ground. The shield fell on top of them.

'What's going on in here?' screamed a voice. A loud, angry, ferocious voice.

Hack and Whack huddled under the shield.

'Do you think it's an ogre?' whispered Hack.

'Or a troll?' whispered Whack.

Maybe it won't notice us, thought Hack.

We're so good at hiding, thought Whack.

The troll/ogre/monster stomped over and yanked up the shield.

'What are you doing?' screamed the troll/ogre/ monster.

'Mum!' said Hack.

'Mum!' said Whack. 'What are **you** doing on Bad Island?'

'Bad Island? What are you talking about?' shouted Mum. 'This is Bear Island, where you live. What are you doing? Get out from under the bench, Twisty Pants and Dirty Ulf. Just wait till I tell your parents!'

Twisty Pants and Dirty Ulf crawled out from under the bench. Bitey-Bitey crawled out from behind the loom.

Hack looked at Whack.

Whack looked at Hack.

They must have sailed the wrong way.

Hack and Whack had raided ... their own home.

Mum glared at them. 'How many times have I told you—'

Suddenly Elsa Gold-Hair burst

in, clutching her mushroom basket.

'Something's strange, I just found my . . .' Her voice trailed off.

Hack snatched Elsa's basket.

'Look, Mum, here's all the mushrooms we gathered, just like you asked,' she said, handing the basket to Mum.

Mum looked confused.

'What's going on, Hack and Whack?'

'Just rushing to do our chores,' said Hack, heading for the door.

'And now we're off to feed the chickens,' said Whack, following her out.

'And we're helping them,' said Twisty Pants, as he scrambled away from Hack's angry mum.

'We love helping friends do their chores,' said Dirty Ulf, scurrying after them.

Elsa Gold-Hair stood still.

She'd spent hours collecting those mushrooms . . .

'What do you have to say, Elsa Gold-Hair?' snapped Mum.

Elsa gulped.

'Enjoy the mushrooms,' said Elsa, then turned and fled.

She joined the terrible Vikings outside the longhouse by the chicken coop.

'C'mon, everybody . . . run!' shrieked Whack. 'Last one to the beach is a rotten herring.'

THE END